THE TALE OF PIGLING BLAND

From the authorized animated series
based on the original tales

BY BEATRIX POTTER™

F. WARNE & Co.

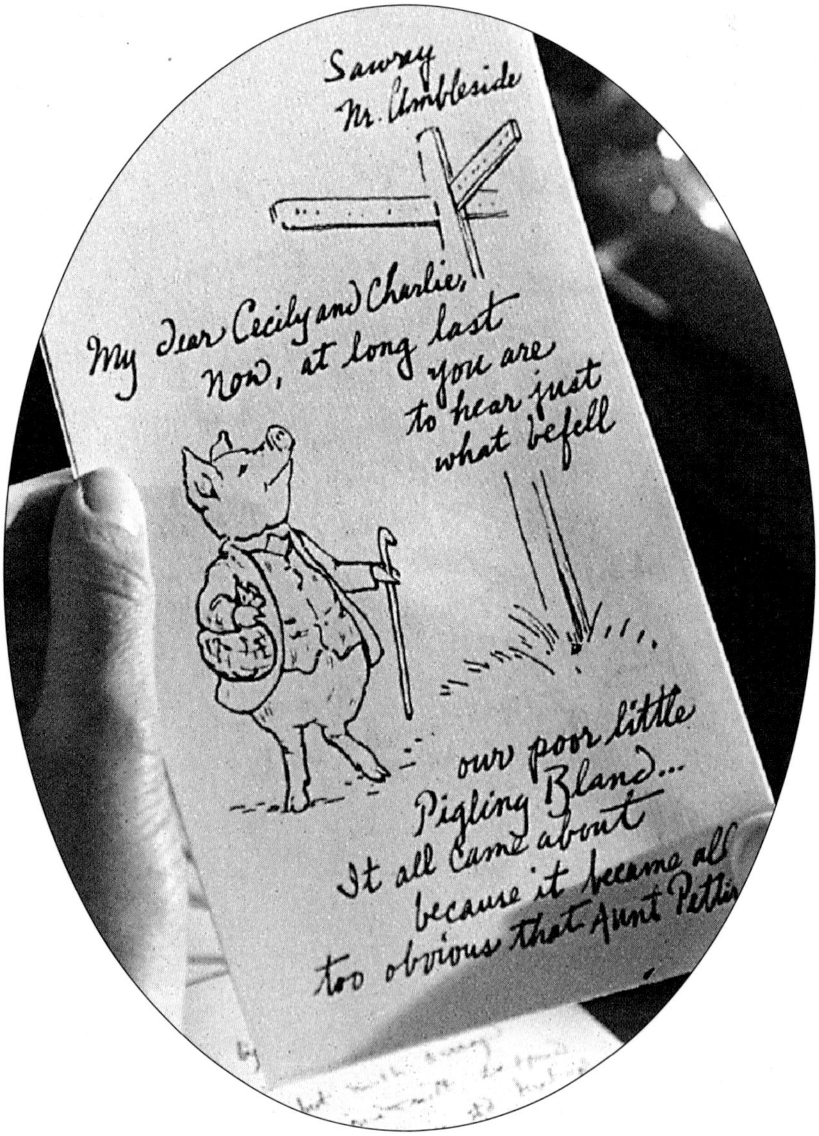

Once upon a time there was an old pig called Aunt Pettitoes.

She had eight of a family; four little girl pigs, called Cross-patch, Suck-suck, Yock-yock and Spot; and four little boy pigs, called Alexander, Pigling Bland, Chin-chin and Stumpy.

The eight little pigs had very fine appetites.

'I do believe I can't be coping much longer with my
unruly brood,' Aunt Pettitoes sighed. 'They are indeed
becoming a burden and a worry. Good little Spot shall stay
at home to do the housework, but the others must go.

'Pigling Bland, you must go to market. You too,
Alexander.'

Aunt Pettitoes handed the two little pigs their licences
permitting them to travel to market.
   'Beware of hen roosts and bacon and eggs,' she warned.
   'Now, take these eight conversation peppermints, and do heed
the moral sentiments on them and you'll come to no harm.'
   Pigling Bland and Alexander set off for market.

The two little pigs trotted along steadily for a mile.

'Let's see what they've given us for dinner, Pigling?' asked Alexander presently.

'If you must,' replied Pigling, 'but isn't it rather soon?'

Alexander gobbled up his dinner in no time, but still feeling rather hungry, asked for one of Pigling's peppermints.

'I wish to preserve them for emergencies,' replied Pigling
Bland, at which Alexander squealed with laughter.

  Then Alexander jumped up to get Pigling's sandwich.
Pigling tumbled to the ground and pieces of paper floated
from his pockets.

  'That's quite enough, Alexander,' he reproved, picking up
the licences.

The two little pigs were trotting along together singing,
'Tom, Tom, the piper's son,' when Pigling stopped abruptly.
 'What's that, young sirs? Stole a pig? Where are your
licences?' the policeman demanded.
 Pigling Bland pulled out his licence and showed it to the
policeman. Alexander pulled a scrumpled piece of paper from
his pocket.

8

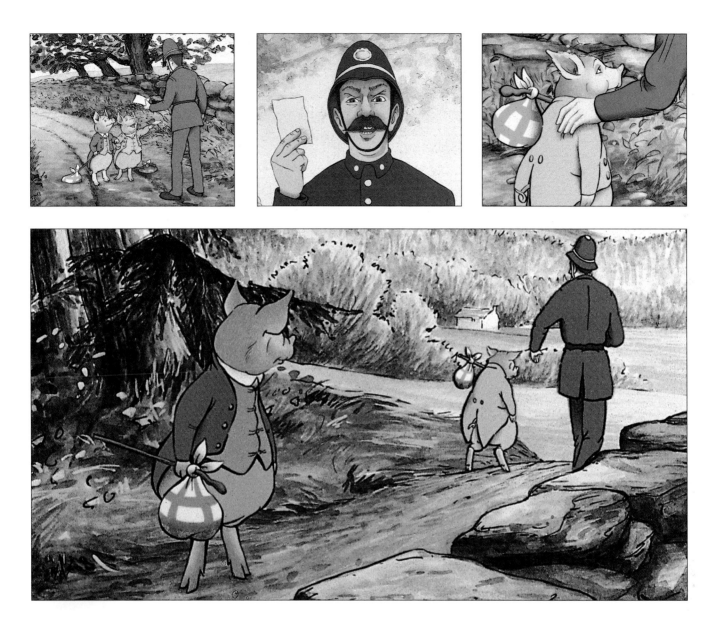

'What's this?' asked the policeman, reading Alexander's paper. 'Two and a half conversation sweeties at three farthings? This ain't a licence!'

'But I had one,' said Alexander. The policeman didn't believe him. 'I'm passing the farm – you may walk back with me,' and then he led Alexander away.

Pigling Bland was left all alone.

Pigling continued on his way dejectedly.

'Oh, I cannot bear the thought of market,' he said
miserably. 'I never wanted to go in the first place. To be
stared at, prodded, then hired by some strange farmer. All I
ever wanted was to have a little garden of my own and
grow potatoes.'

Pigling pulled his jacket tightly round his neck, and put his hands in his pockets to warm them.

'What's this?' he wondered, finding some papers.

'Alexander's licence!'

He turned back and started to run. 'Alexander!' he called. 'Oh – I might just overtake them – Mr Policeman, I've found the licence.'

But Pigling Bland took several wrong turns and very soon
he was quite lost. The wind whistled and the trees creaked
and Pigling began to feel frightened.

'I can't find my way home!' he cried. 'Wherever can I
be? I must find somewhere to rest for the night.'

Then, past the edge of the wood, he saw a small wooden
hut and crept inside.

It was a hen roost. Pigling squeezed between two hens.
 'Bacon and eggs! Bacon and eggs!' the hens shrieked.
 'It is only a hen house, but what can I do? I must leave no later than daybreak,' resolved Pigling, feeling rather alarmed. He curled up and fell fast asleep.

In less than an hour, the door creaked open and a bright light
shone into Pigling's face. It was the farmer, Mr Piperson.

'I need six of you fowl to take to market in the morning,'
he whispered to himself, grabbing a hen roughly.

'Here's another,' said Mr Piperson gleefully, catching sight
of Pigling.

Then he dropped five more dirty, kicking, cackling hens upon the top of Pigling Bland.

Back at the farm kitchen, Mr Piperson opened the lid of
the hamper and lifted Pigling out.

'I am but a poor little pig,' explained Pigling, showing
his empty pockets at the farmer's request.

'You'll stay for supper?' asked the farmer.

'Yes,' replied Pigling nervously. 'Thank you kindly.'

Mr Piperson pulled off his boots and threw them to a corner.
As they hit the wainscot there was a smothered noise. Indeed,
it seemed to Pigling that something at the further end
of the kitchen was taking a suppressed interest in the cooking.
  Mr Piperson poured out three platefuls of porridge: one for
himself, one for Pigling and a *third*.

Pigling ate his porridge discreetly.

After supper Mr Piperson consulted an almanac and looked at Pigling Bland intently.

Then he prodded Pigling's ribs.

'It's too late in the season for curing bacon,' he muttered to
himself, glancing at the small remains of a ham strung
from the rafters.

Then he turned to Pigling.

'Oh well, you may sleep on the rug.'

'You'll likely be moving on again?' Mr Piperson asked
Pigling Bland the next morning. Before Pigling could
answer there was a whistle from outside. It was
Mr Piperson's neighbour to take him to market.
   'Now, don't meddle with nought, or I'll skin ye!' said Mr
Piperson menacingly.
   Pigling watched the cart turn the corner.

Back inside, Pigling finished off his breakfast and began to sing to himself. Suddenly a little smothered voice chimed in.

Pigling listened carefully and started to search for the voice. He came to the locked cupboard and pushed a peppermint under the door. It was sucked in immediately.

'Ah ha,' said Pigling. 'Very interesting.'

Mr Piperson returned from market and made some
porridge for himself and Pigling.

But Mr Piperson was tired and soon made his way to
bed. Pigling Bland sat alone by the fire, finishing his
supper, when all at once a little voice spoke –

'My name is Pig-wig. Make me some more porridge,
please!'

'I'm Pigling Bland,' replied Pigling rather startled. 'Er, more porridge? Of course. How did you escape?'

   'He forgot to lock the cupboard,' Pig-wig replied.

   'How did you come here?'

   'Stolen,' said Pig-wig with her mouth full.

   'What for?' enquired Pigling; to which Pig-wig replied, 'Bacon, hams.'

'But why don't you run away?'

'I will,' Pig-wig answered, 'after supper.'

But Pig-wig didn't seem to know her way home.

'I'm going to market and I have two pig papers. I might take you to the bridge,' Pigling offered, 'if you have no objection.'

'How wonderfully kind!' exclaimed Pig-wig thankfully.

Pigling told Pig-wig all about market and how he would much rather have his own little garden.

'I love flowers!' Pig-wig exclaimed.

'Potatoes,' corrected Pigling.

Pig-wig began to sing a little tune. With each verse her head nodded lower and her little twinkly eyes closed up. Soon she was fast asleep.

Early the next morning Pigling woke Pig-wig.

    'Come along, Pig-wig. It's time for us to be on our way,' he whispered.

    'But it's so dark,' complained Pig-wig.

    'Come away,' urged Pigling. 'We will be able to see when we get used to it!'

Pigling Bland and Pig-wig slipped away, hand in hand,
across an untidy field to the road.

Presently, Pig-wig asked, 'Why do you want to go to
market, Pigling?'

'I don't want,' he replied. 'I want to grow potatoes.'

They continued along the lane when suddenly Pigling
caught sight of a ploughman in the nearby field.

'Keep under the wall!' he whispered. 'Not far now. We'll
soon be safe and sound across the boundary.'

Slowly bumping along the road came the grocer's cart.

'Take that peppermint out of your mouth,' instructed Pigling. 'We may have to run. Don't say a word. Leave it to me.'

'Where are you two going?' demanded the grocer. 'Are you going to market? Show me your licences.'

The grocer studied the licences.

'I'm not sure,' he said uncertainly, taking a good look at Pig-wig. 'This here pig is a young lady pig.'

He opened his newspaper at the 'Lost, Stolen or Strayed' section. 'Ten shillings reward,' he muttered thoughtfully.

'Wait here,' he commanded and went to consult the ploughman.

Pigling and Pig-wig waited for a moment - and then off
they raced! They reached the bridge and crossed it hand in
hand.

　'Freedom! Safety!' cried Pigling happily.

　'You shall have your garden, full of potatoes,' said
Pig-wig with delight.

　'*And* pansies!' added Pigling.

Then over the hills and far away, Pig-wig danced with
Pigling Bland. As they danced they sang a tune:
  'Tom, Tom the piper's son,
  Stole a pig and away he ran
  And all the tune that he could play
  Was *over the hills and far away*!'